ONCE UPON A TIME . . .

. . . a carpenter picked up a strange lump of wood while mending a table. When he began to whittle it, the wood started to moan. The frightened carpenter decided to get rid of it at once. He gave it to his friend, the cobbler Geppetto, who wanted to make a puppet.

"I'll call him Pinocchio," mused the cobbler. "That's a lucky name." Back in his workshop, Geppetto started to carve the wood.

Suddenly a voice squealed, "Ooh! That hurt!"

Geppetto was astonished. Excitement mounting, he carved a head, then eyes that immediately stared right at the cobbler. But the moment Geppetto carved the nose, it grew longer and longer, no matter how often the cobbler cut it down to size.

The newly carved mouth began to chuckle. "Be still," scolded Geppetto, but the puppet rudely stuck out his tongue. By the time the cobbler had shaped the hands and feet, the wooden puppet was ready to snatch off the good man's wig and give him a hearty kick.

"You naughty boy!" said Geppetto reproachfully. "I haven't even finished making you, yet you have no respect for me — your father!" Nevertheless, the kind old fellow picked up the puppet, and, a step at a time, taught him to walk. But the minute Pinocchio could manage his legs he ran wildly about the room, then out the door and into the street.

"Stop him! Stop him!" shouted the cobbler. The passers-by just laughed.

Luckily, a policeman heard the cobbler's shouts and quickly grabbed the runaway, handing him over to his father.

"I'll box your ears!" gasped Geppetto. But that wasn't possible, for he had forgotten to carve ears for the puppet.

"I'm sorry, father," said Pinocchio, who had been frightened by the policeman.

Geppetto forgave his son and carved him a pair of ears — although they were only half-finished, because Pinocchio wriggled so much. The cobbler also made Pinocchio a jacket of flowered paper, a pair of plain trousers, some bark shoes, and a bread hat.

"How smart I look!" said Pinocchio, hugging his father. "I'd like to go to school so I can help you when you're old."

"What a thoughtful boy," said Geppetto. "But we haven't enough money even to buy a first reader." Pinocchio's mouth drooped. Geppetto suddenly rose, put on his old coat, and left the house. Soon he returned, carrying a first reader, but minus his coat. It was snowing outside.

"Where's your coat, father?"

"I sold it because it kept me too warm."

Pinocchio threw his arms around Geppetto's neck and kissed the kindly old man.

It had stopped snowing, and Pinocchio set out for school with his reader tucked under his arm, full of good intentions. "Today I'll learn to read, tomorrow to write, and the next day I'll learn to count," he said to himself. "Then I'll earn the money for a new coat for Geppetto . . ." But alas, the sound of a brass band broke into the puppet's daydream, and he forgot all about school.

In the town square, people were clustering around a brightly-colored booth.

"What's that?" Pinocchio asked a bystander.

"Can't you read the sign? It says: *Great Puppet Show: Four Pennies a Person.*"

"Who'll give me four pennies for this brand new book?" Pinocchio cried. A junk dealer quickly bought the reader, and Pinocchio hurried into the booth. Poor Geppetto, his sacrifice had been quite in vain!

Hardly had Pinocchio got inside than the puppets on stage began to shout, "Pinocchio! Come and join us. Hurray for brother Pinocchio!" Of course the giddy boy rushed onto the stage and chattered with his new friends. The spectators began to mutter.

Out strode the puppet master, Giovanni, a hulking man with a long black beard and bushy eyebrows that made him look very fierce indeed.

"What's going on here!" he roared. "Stop that noise or you'll hear about it later on!"

That evening, when Giovanni sat down to dinner, he found his mutton half-cooked. "Humph! The stove needs more wood. Come here, Pinocchio. At least you're good for something!"

The poor puppet burst into tears. "Save me, father! I don't want to die!"

Giovanni was quite taken aback. "You have parents?" he asked.

"A father — but I never knew a mother," said the puppet in a low voice.

The big man's heart melted. "Well, I'll take pity on your father," he said, "but I must finish roasting the mutton. Bring me Harlequin!"

When Pinocchio saw that another puppet would be burned instead, he cried harder the ever. "Oh, please don't burn Harlequin!"

"Enough!" boomed Giovanni. "I want my meat properly cooked."

"In that case, burn me," said Pinocchio defiantly.

Giovanni was dumbfounded. "Well, well! I've never met a puppet hero before! I might just . . ." Hope flooded through Pinocchio as the puppeteer stared at him. At last the man said, "All right, I'll eat half-raw mutton tonight, but next time somebody will find himself in a pickle!"

The puppeteer asked about Pinocchio's father. "Here, take these to him," he said, handing the wooden boy five gold pieces, "and tell him to buy a warm new coat."

Pinocchio thanked Giovanni and cheerfully left the puppet booth. He was hurrying homeward when he met with a half-blind cat and a lame fox. He told them all about his good fortune. The pair peered greedily at the gold coins.

"If you'd really like to please your father," said the crafty fox, "we know of a meadow where you can sow these five coins. The next day, you'll find ten times as many!"

The gullible puppet followed the limping fox and the cat, who led him to the edge of a meadow.

"See that big dead tree?" said the fox. "You must dig a hole at the foot of it, and bury your gold. We'll wait here."

Night was falling, when Pinocchio set off. Before he had gone very far, two hooded shapes loomed up. "Your money or your life!" growled one in a suspiciously foxy voice.

The puppet had hidden the gold coins under his tongue and couldn't speak. He stared in silent fear.

"We'll see about that!" said the angry robbers, tying Pinocchio to a tree. The wicked pair then sneaked away. Pinocchio thought miserably of his father.

As luck would have it, a fairy passed by and saw the hapless puppet. "Whatever happened?" she asked, clapping her hands for her pet woodpeckers. The birds pecked the rope to pieces. Thump! Pinocchio sat down hard and nearly swallowed the coins. He quickly put them in his pocket for safekeeping.

In answer to the fairy's question, Pinocchio told his story, but left out the part about selling the reader. His nose began to get longer and longer.

"Goodness, you must be fibbing!" laughed the fairy. "I can tell because your nose is growing." She clapped her hands again, and the woodpeckers came and pecked Pinocchio's nose down to size.

"Go straight home to your father, now," scolded the fairy, as they parted. But foolish Pinocchio buried the coins at the foot of the tree. He waited under a bush until dawn, then hurried back, only to find an empty hole!

9

Pinocchio trudged sadly home. Geppetto was overjoyed, and again forgave his son's thoughtlessness. Pinocchio set off for school once more, full of good intentions. Alas, there he met Carlo, the lazybones of the class.

"Why don't you come to Toyland with me?" said Carlo. "Nobody ever studies there, and you can play all day long!"

"Does such a place really exist?" asked Pinocchio in amazement.

"The wagon is coming by this evening to take me there. Would you like to come?"

Forgetting all his good intentions, Pinocchio joined his newfound friend. Midnight struck and the wagon arrived, filled with boisterous schoolboys. Twelve pairs of sad little donkeys wearing boots pulled the wagon. Pinocchio was too excited to notice any of this, and clambered up on the back of a donkey. "Hurray! We're off!" he shouted.

Toyland was just as Carlo had predicted. No one was even allowed to whisper the word "school".

"This is the life!" Pinocchio exclaimed whenever he met Carlo.

"I was right, wasn't I?" said his friend smugly.

One day, however, Pinocchio awoke to a nasty surprise. When he raised a hand to his head, he found he'd sprouted a long pair of hairy ears! By the next day, they were longer than ever.

Pinocchio pulled on a large cotton cap and went off in search of his friend. Carlo had on a hat pulled right down to his nose. The two boys stared at each other, then snatched off their hats, roaring with laughter at the funny sight.

But as they laughed, Carlo suddenly went pale and began to stagger. "Pinocchio, help!" But Pinocchio himself was stumbling about, and he burst into tears as he felt himself go down on all fours. Pinocchio and Carlo were turning into a pair of donkeys! They tried to groan with fear, but brayed loudly instead.

When the Toyland wagon driver heard the braying of his new donkeys, he rubbed his hands in glee. "Two fine new donkeys for market. I'll get at least four gold pieces for them!" Such was the awful fate that awaited boys who played hooky!

The wagon driver sold Pinocchio for two gold pieces to a leather-maker. The tanner tied a rope around the donkey's foot and led it to a cliff, as the poor animal looked at the waves, the man kicked it over the edge!

Pinocchio struggled with all his might, thinking desperately of his father. Suddenly a school of little fish appeared and began to nibble away at the donkey-skin. Just as they'd finished, Pinocchio felt himself being hauled up by the leg.

"Where's my donkey skin?" gasped the tanner, lunging at Pinocchio.

"That was me!" giggled Pinocchio nervously, nimbly slipping his foot out of the rope.

"Two gold coins for a stick!" shouted the tanner angrily. "I'll sell you for firewood."

"Oh no you won't," said Pinocchio. With a twist and a leap he dodged the tanner and dove head first into the sea.

It so happened that, at this very moment, a huge whale came gliding by, jaws wide open to catch anything in its path.

"Help!" cried Pinocchio, swimming as hard as he could. But a wave washed him into the cavernous mouth, and down he went, tossed in the torrent of water that poured down the whale's throat.

When Pinocchio came to his senses, everything was pitch black. Overhead he could hear the loud heave of the whale's gills. The puppet crept on all fours along what seemed like a sloping path, crying as he went, "Help! Won't anybody save me?"

Suddenly a flickering light appeared ahead. And what was that? A battered table and chair? A candle stuck in a bottle? And a man —

"Father! Is it really you!"

"Pinocchio! Son!"

Sobbing for joy, they hugged each other. Geppetto stroked the puppet's head and told how he came to be in the whale's stomach.

"When I couldn't find you on land, I made a boat to search for you on the sea. But the boat sank in a storm, and the whale gulped me down. Luckily, it also swallowed bits of shipwreck, so I've managed to survive."

"We must get out of here!" urged Pinocchio, taking Geppetto's hand.

"I think the whale should be asleep now," said Geppetto. The pair started to climb up the whale's stomach, using a candle to light the way. They crept along the whale's tongue and right up to its teeth. The heat of the candle and the tickling of their feet made the whale restless.

"Hang on!" cried Geppetto, dropping his candle and clinging to Pinocchio.

"A-a-gh-h-h!" The whale, stung by the pain of the burning candle, spat out its victims with such force that they flew through the air. Pinocchio and Geppetto landed in the breakers by the shore.

On the beach stood an old hut, and there they took shelter. Geppetto seemed ill and weak from hunger.

"I'm going to get you some milk," said Pinocchio. The bleating of goats led the puppet in the right direction, and he soon came upon a farmer. Of course, he had no money to pay for the milk.

"My donkey's dead," said the farmer. "If you work the treadmill from dawn to dusk, you can have some milk." And so, for days on end, Pinocchio rose early each morning to earn Geppetto's food.

At long last, Pinocchio and Geppetto reached home. The puppet worked late into the night weaving reed baskets to make money for his father and himself.

One night, in a wonderful dream, the fairy appeared to reward Pinocchio for his kindness. The next morning, Pinocchio rose as usual. But when he looked in the mirror, he couldn't believe his eyes. There he was, a real flesh and blood boy with sparkling blue eyes, real hair, and . . . a small nose!

Geppetto gasped when he saw his son, a real boy at last. He hugged him happily.

"What happened to my old wooden self?" wondered Pinocchio.

"There!" exclaimed Geppetto, pointing to a form slumped on a chair. "I couldn't carve a heart for the old Pinocchio, but because of your hard work and kindness, you made one for yourself!"